W9-BGL-531

Dear Parents:

Congratulations! Your child is taking the first steps on an exciting journey. The destination? Independent reading!

STEP INTO READING® will help your child get there. The program offers five steps to reading success. Each step includes fun stories and colorful art or photographs. In addition to original fiction and books with favorite characters, there are Step into Reading Non-Fiction Readers, Phonics Readers and Boxed Sets, Sticker Readers, and Comic Readers—a complete literacy program with something to interest every child.

Learning to Read, Step by Step!

Ready to Read **Preschool–Kindergarten**
• big type and easy words • rhyme and rhythm • picture clues
For children who know the alphabet and are eager to begin reading.

Reading with Help **Preschool–Grade 1**
• basic vocabulary • short sentences • simple stories
For children who recognize familiar words and sound out new words with help.

Reading on Your Own **Grades 1–3**
• engaging characters • easy-to-follow plots • popular topics
For children who are ready to read on their own.

Reading Paragraphs **Grades 2–3**
• challenging vocabulary • short paragraphs • exciting stories
For newly independent readers who read simple sentences with confidence.

Ready for Chapters **Grades 2–4**
• chapters • longer paragraphs • full-color art
For children who want to take the plunge into chapter books but still like colorful pictures.

STEP INTO READING® is designed to give every child a successful reading experience. The grade levels are only guides; children will progress through the steps at their own speed, developing confidence in their reading.

Remember, a lifetime love of reading starts with a single step!

For rugrats Brayden and Jason

—C. B. C.

Published in the United States by Random House Children's Books, a division of Penguin Random House LLC, 1745 Broadway, New York, NY 10019, and in Canada by Penguin Random House Canada Limited, Toronto.

Step into Reading, Random House, and the Random House colophon are registered trademarks of Penguin Random House LLC.

Visit us on the Web!
StepIntoReading.com
rhcbooks.com

Educators and librarians, for a variety of teaching tools, visit us at RHTeachersLibrarians.com

ISBN 978-0-593-43181-8 (trade) — ISBN 978-0-593-43182-5 (lib. bdg.)

Printed in the United States of America

10 9 8 7 6 5 4 3 2 1

STEP INTO READING®

nickelodeon

by Courtney Carbone
based on the teleplay by Jeff D'Elia
illustrated by Erik Doescher

Random House New York

A space convention was in town!
It was based on the movie
Final Eclipse.

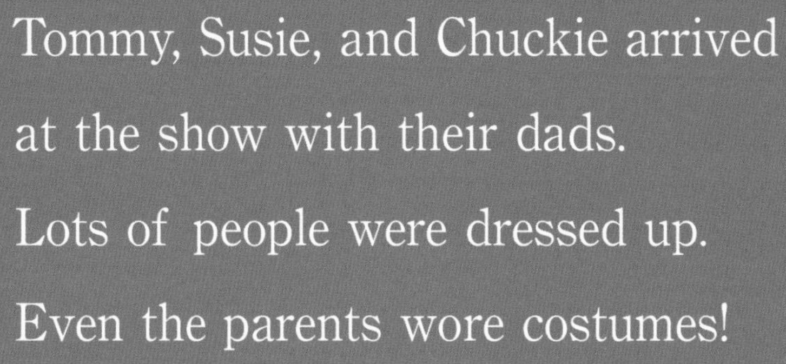

Tommy, Susie, and Chuckie arrived
at the show with their dads.
Lots of people were dressed up.
Even the parents wore costumes!

“We are going to the next galaxy!”
Susie cheered.
The babies went on a ride
with their parents.
It looked like a spaceship.

General Jade O'Neil
appeared on a screen.
She was Susie's favorite hero!
"We hear you loud and weird,"
Susie said.

The general warned everyone
that a villain was on the loose!
His name was Lord Crater.
The general told them
about a special mind power.
It was called the Alpha.

Susie explained the Alpha.
"Bad guys crumble before
your eyes," she said.
Tommy and Chuckie listened.
They all wanted to be ready
for Lord Crater.

Suddenly, Lord Crater appeared on the screen.

Boom!

He tried to blast their spaceship out of the sky!

The vehicle bounced and shook.
The general came to the rescue.
They narrowly escaped
as the ride slowed to a halt.

Now it was time for a screening
of the new *Final Eclipse* trailer.
The theater guard was
dressed as an evil henchman.
The babies thought
he was called a *stenchman.*

Tommy's dad could not find the tickets.

"No tickets, no entry,"

said the guard.

Susie's dad had an idea.
He tried to run
past the henchman.
His plan did not work.

Everyone was sent
to a waiting room instead.
"The stenchmen are madder,"
Chuckie said. "I hope they
do not get stinkier!"

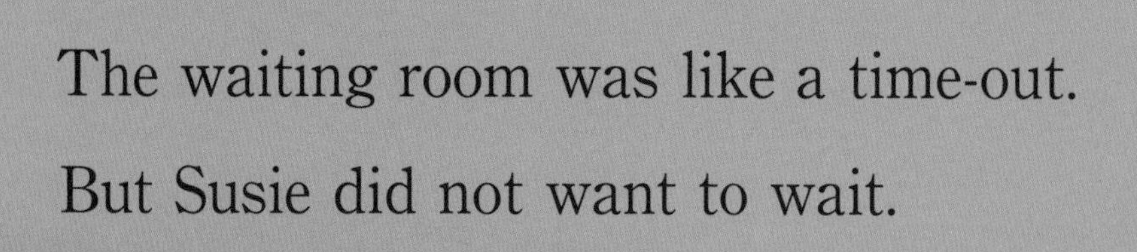

The waiting room was like a time-out.

But Susie did not want to wait.

She wanted to find Lord Crater.

The babies went
looking for him.

The babies wanted costumes, too.
They dressed as alien creatures
called borfballs.
It was a good disguise.
They fit right in!

Soon they spotted Lord Crater.

The babies followed Lord Crater through the showroom.

They ended up on a wobbly bridge.

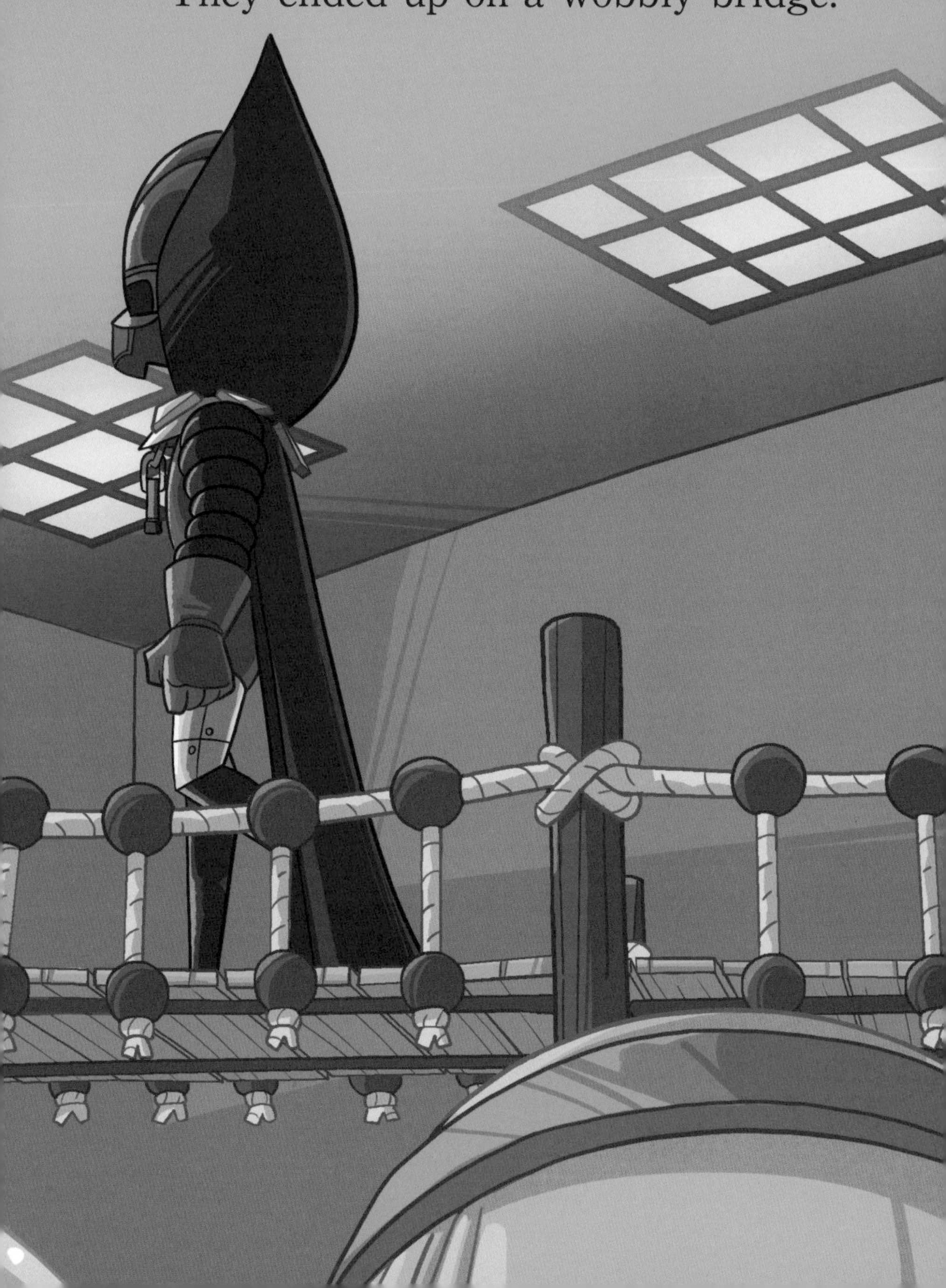

“I have a tiny fear
of plunging to my doom,”
said Chuckie.
“Take my hand,” said Tommy.

The babies all held hands.

They slowly crossed the bridge.

It swayed back and forth.

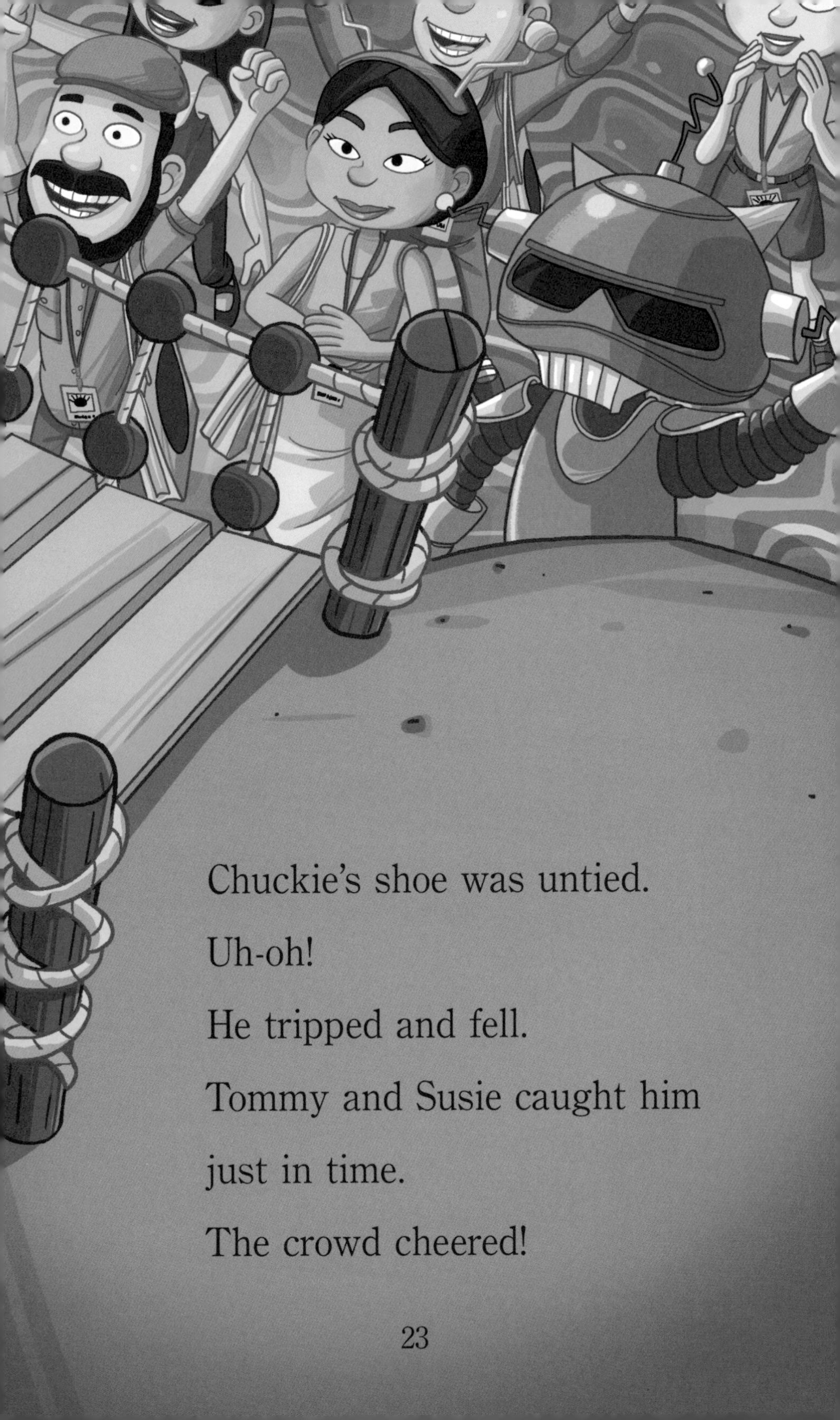

Chuckie's shoe was untied.

Uh-oh!

He tripped and fell.

Tommy and Susie caught him just in time.

The crowd cheered!

Lord Crater was getting away.
The babies had to
find a way to catch up.
"We cannot give up now,"
Susie said.

The babies saw a shiny object.
It was a go-kart
that looked like a spaceship.
They quickly hopped inside.
It was time to hit the space highway!

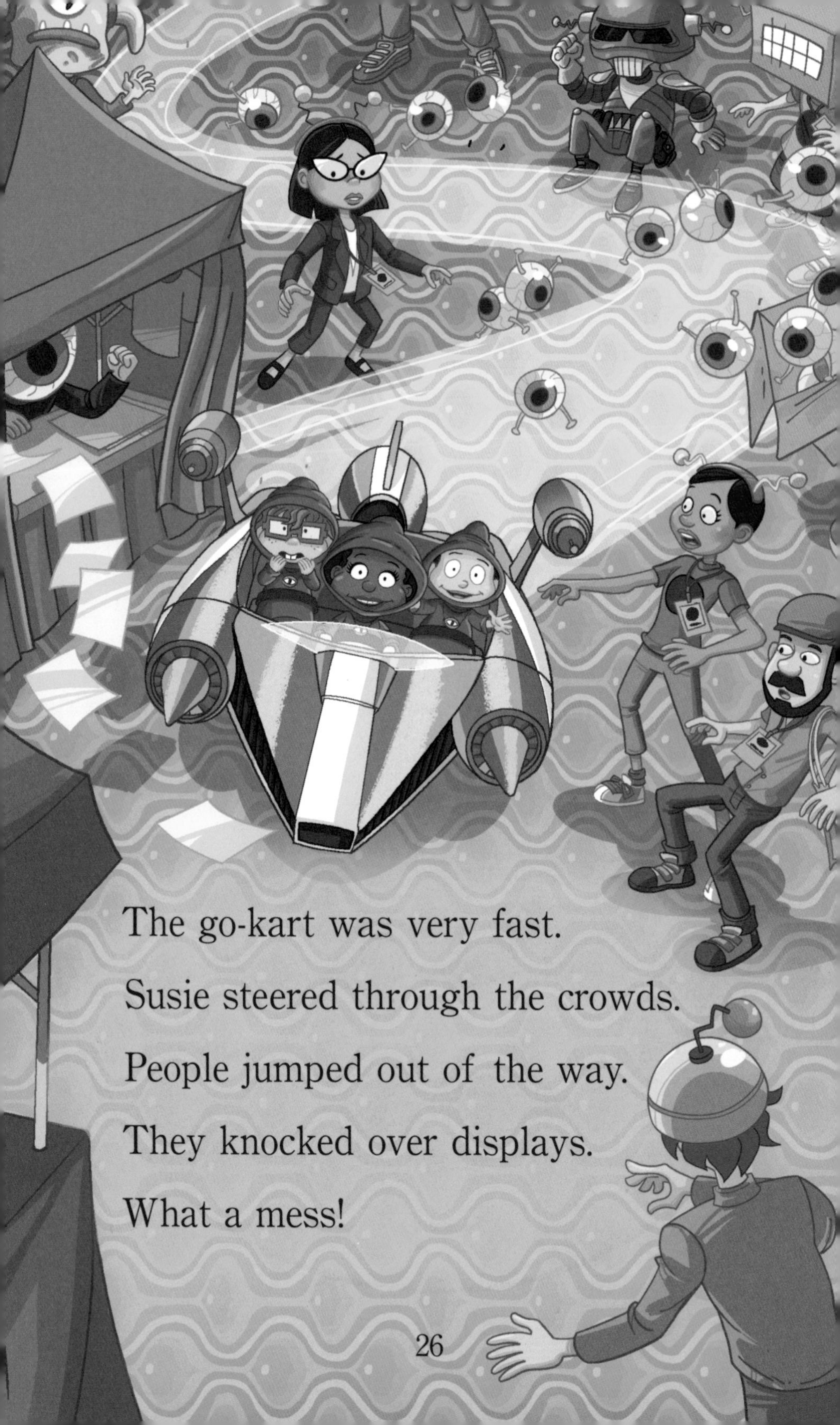

The go-kart was very fast.

Susie steered through the crowds.

People jumped out of the way.

They knocked over displays.

What a mess!

The guards spotted the babies.

"The stenchmen saw us!"
Chuckie cried.

"Do not worry," Susie replied.
"I am going to lose them!"

Lord Crater appeared
before a large crowd.
Beep, beep!
The babies drove
right up to him.
Lord Crater was confused.
The babies did the Alpha.

It worked!

Lord Crater played along.

He crumpled to the floor.

The crowd cheered again.

The parents came running.

They saw what had happened.

"Our kids saved the universe!"
said Tommy's dad.
"I have never been so proud,"
added Susie's dad.

Mission accomplished!